JESUS MADE A MARVELOUS ME

A *Jesus in My Little Pocket* Book

I will sing for joy about what
your hands have done.

Psalm 92:4

S0-CRS-764

Thomas Nelson Publishers
Nashville

Jesus made a marvelous me...

He made me to
love Him and
to serve Him.

The Word says...

You must not have any other gods
except me.

Exodus 20:3

Fold Here

- -

FROM: _____

TO: ——————

——————————

Jesus made a marvelous me...

He made my
eyes for seeing
the beautiful
colors in a rain-
bow, and for
reading His
good news.

The Word says...

Good news makes you feel better.

Your happiness will show in your eyes.

Proverbs 15:30

With L♥V

Jesus in My Little Pocket

- - - - - - - - - - - - - - - Fold Here - - - - - - - - - - - - - - - - - - -

FROM: _____

TO: _____

_____

Jesus made a marvelous me...

He wants me to be brave. Even when I'm afraid, I know Jesus is watching over me.

The Word says...

Good people are as brave as a lion.

Proverbs 28:1

7

With ♥ LOVE

Jesus in My Little Pocket

- - - - - - - - - - - Fold Here - - - - - - - - - - - - - -

FROM: _____

TO: —————————

—————————

Jesus made a marvelous me...

He made my
laugh and my
special giggle.

The Word says...

A happy heart is like good medicine.

Proverbs 17:22

With Love

Jesus in My Little Pocket

------------------ Fold Here ------------------

FROM: _____

TO: _____

_____

Jesus made a marvelous me...

He wants me to
be kind. I treat
people and ani-
mals and all
living things as
Jesus treats me.

The Word says...

Do for other people the same things you
want them to do for you.

Matthew 7:12

With L♥V

Jesus in My Little Pocket

--------------------- Fold Here ---------------------

FROM: _____

TO: ———————

———————

Jesus made a marvelous me...

He made my
tears and He
hears me when I
cry.

The Word says...

The Lord hears good people when they
cry out to him.

He saves them from all their troubles.

Psalm 34:17

13

With L♥V

Jesus in My Little Pocket

- - - - - - - - - - - - - - Fold Here - - - - - - - - - - - - - - -

FROM: _____

TO: _____

_____

Jesus made a marvelous me...

He wants me to
be a good friend
to others, even
when they are
not friendly to
me.

The Word says...

Love your neighbor as you love yourself.

Mark 12:31

15

With L♥V

Jesus in My Little Pocket

-------------------------------- Fold Here --------------------------------

FROM: _____

TO: ———————

_____

Jesus made a marvelous me...

He made my hands for clap-ping when I'm glad.

The Word says...

Clap your hands, all you people.

Shout to God with joy.

Psalm 47:1

With L♥V
Jesus in My Little Pocket

- - - - - - - - - - - - - - Fold Here - - - - - - - - - - - - - -

FROM: _____

TO: ——————
_____

Jesus made a marvelous me...

He wants me to
be happy and
joyful.

The Word says...

Happy are the people who know how to
    praise you.
  Lord, let them live in the light of your
    presence.

Psalm 89:15

19

Jesus in My Little Pocket

With L♥V

-- Fold Here --

FROM: _____

TO: —————

_____

Jesus made a marvelous me...

He made my
hair exactly as
He thought it
should be—
curly or
straight, blonde
or brown or
black or red.

The Word says...

Christ gave each one of us a special gift.
Each one received what Christ wanted to
give him.

Ephesians 4:7

With L♥VE

Jesus in My Little Pocket

----------------------------------- Fold Here -----------------------------------

FROM: _____

TO: ——————

_____

Jesus made a marvelous me...

He wants me to be forgiving, especially when someone has hurt my feelings.

The Word says...

Be kind and loving to each other. Forgive each other just as God forgave you in Christ.

Ephesians 4:32

------- Fold Here -------

FROM: _____

TO: ———————

_____

Jesus made a marvelous me...

**He made my
feet for dancing.**

The Word says...

They should praise him with dancing.

They should praise him with

tambourines and harps.

Psalm 149:3

25

With L♥V

-------- Fold Here --------------------------

FROM: _____

TO: _____

_____

Jesus made a marvelous me...

He wants me to
be honest.

The Word says...

Do not wrong your brother or cheat him.

1 Thessalonians 4:6

27

Fold Here

FROM: _____

TO: ————————

————————

Jesus made a marvelous me...

He made my
arms for giving
hugs.

The Word says...

Jesus took the children in his arms. He
put his hands on them and blessed them.

Mark 10:16

29

With L♥♥V

Jesus in My Little Pocket

---------- Fold Here ----------

FROM: _____

TO: —————————

_____

Jesus made a marvelous me...

He wants me to
be thankful. Not
only for the
food I eat, but
for my friends,
my family and
for the beautiful
earth on which I live.

The Word says...

Always give thanks to God the Father for
everything, in the name of our Lord Jesus
Christ.

Ephesians 5:20

With Love

Jesus in My Little Pocket

Fold Here

FROM: _____

TO: _____

_____

Jesus made a marvelous me...

He made my voice for singing hymns of praise to Him.

The Word says...

If one of you is happy, he should sing praises.

James 5:13

With ♥♥ 💜
Jesus in My Little Pocket

----------------------------- **Fold Here** -----------------------------

FROM: _____

TO: ———

_____

Jesus made a marvelous me...

He wants me to
be giving.

The Word says...

The way you give to others is the way
God will give to you.

Mark 4:24

35

With 💜
Jesus in My Little Pocket

------------------------- Fold Here -------------------------

FROM: _____

TO: ————

————

Jesus made a marvelous me...

He made my
nose for
smelling flowers
and cookies,
fresh from the
oven.

The Word says...

When I was put together...

> you saw my body as it was formed.

Psalm 139:15-16

37

TO: _____

_____

FROM: _____

_____

- -
Fold Here

With L♥V
Jesus in My Little Pocket

Jesus made a marvelous me...

He wants me to
be bright and
full of light, and
He reminds me
not to hide
from the world.

The Word says...

You are the light that gives light to the
world.

Matthew 5:14

Jesus in My Little Pocket

With Love ♥

Fold Here

FROM: _____

TO: ——————————

_____

Jesus made a marvelous me...

He made my
tummy to fill
with good
things to eat!

The Word says...

God fills the hungry with good things.

Luke 1:53

With L♥V

Jesus in My Little Pocket

------------------------- Fold Here -------------------------

FROM: _____

TO: _____

_____

Jesus made a marvelous me...

He wants me to
be peaceful and
prayerful.

The Word says...

All your children will be taught by the
> Lord.
>> And they will have much peace.

Isaiah 54:13

43

With L♥V

Jesus in My Little Pocket

------------------------ Fold Here ------------------------

FROM: _____

TO: —————————

———————————

Jesus made a marvelous me...

He made my
knees for kneel-
ing when I
pray.

The Word says...

Come, let's bow down and worship him.

Let's kneel before the Lord who

made us.

Psalm 95:6

- - - - - - - - - - - Fold Here - - - - - - - - - - -

FROM: _____

TO: _____

_____

Jesus made a marvelous me...

He wants me to
be obedient, not
only to the
adults in my life
but especially to
Him.

The Word says...

How can a young person live a pure life?

He can do it by obeying your word.

Psalm 119:9

47

- - - - - - - - - - - - - Fold Here - - - - - - - - - - - - - - -

FROM: _____

TO: ————

_____

Jesus made a marvelous me...

And He made people to care for me while I'm on earth.

The Word says...

Honor your father and your mother. Then you will live a long time in the land.

Exodus 20:12

------------------------------ Fold Here ------------------------------

FROM: _____

TO: ——————

_____

Jesus made a marvelous me...

He wants me to be helpful to others.

The Word says...

My children, our love should not be only words and talk. Our love must be true love. And we should show that love by what we do.

1 John 3:18

51

With L♥ve

Jesus in My Little Pocket

---------------------------- Fold Here ----------------------------

FROM: _____

TO: —————

——————————

Jesus made a marvelous me...

He made me
part of His
family. As a
Christian, I
share fellowship
with Him.

The Word says...

The fellowship we share together is with
God the Father and his Son, Jesus Christ.

1 John 1:3

With Love

Jesus in My Little Pocket

---------------- Fold Here ----------------

FROM: _____

TO: ———————

_____

Jesus made a marvelous me...

He wants me to
be truthful.
Even when I
feel like telling a
lie, I know Jesus
wouldn't like it.

The Word says...

He sent Jesus to bless you by turning each
of you away from doing evil things.

Acts 3:26

Jesus in My Little Pocket

With L♥VE

Fold Here

FROM: _____

TO: _____

_____

Jesus made a marvelous me...

He made me special. All my talents were given to me by Him.

The Word says...

Christ gave you a special gift. . . . The gift he gave you teaches you about everything.

1 John 2:27

57

Jesus in My Little Pocket

With L♥V

- Fold Here -

FROM: _____

TO: ———

———

Jesus made a marvelous me...

He wants me to
be courageous. I
have courage
when I feel
afraid because
Jesus is listening
to my prayers
for help.

The Word says...

Remember that I commanded you to be
strong and brave. So don't be afraid. The
Lord your God will be with you every-
where you go.

Joshua 1:9

With ♥ LOVE

Jesus in My Little Pocket

------------------------Fold Here------------------------

FROM: _____

TO: —————
_____

Jesus made a marvelous me...

He made my mouth for talking, and laughing, and praising His name.

The Word says...

It is good to praise the Lord,
　　to sing praises to God Most High.

Psalm 92:1

With Love

Jesus in My Little Pocket

Fold Here

FROM: _____

TO: _____

_____

Jesus made a marvelous me...

He wants me to
be holy, because
I am a child of
God.

The Word says...

The Father has loved us so much! He
loved us so much that we are called
children of God.

1 John 3:1

63

To accept Jesus Christ as your personal Lord and Savior, pray out loud:

Father God, because I believe that Jesus was Your Son, died on the Cross and was raised from the dead for me and my sins, I am saved!